# 最後的咖啡
## The Last Coffee

在轟炸下
在恨如雨下喝咖啡
唯一繼續持有
且快樂有趣的事是，
在他住宿的
混凝土瓦礫間
喝咖啡時
水慢慢開始煮開，
咖啡香味，
使他
感到幸福

（塞爾維亞）艾薇拉‧辜柔維琪（Elvira Kujovic）◎著
李魁賢（Lee Kuei-shien）◎譯

# 自序

艾薇拉‧辜柔維琪 Elvira Kujovic

親愛的讀者，你還沒有讀另外一本書，我能對你說什麼呢？

也許只是我獨特的一些相關資料，也許不是，但對你們有些人來說，應該很熟悉。

我想像得到，有許多人在同一天出生，所以我也希望那些人和我一樣，心裡懷著同樣的愛。

這本書裡有我的心，連同我的心靈。

讀這本書時，你當會瞭解我赤裸的心。

赤裸裸，沒有羞恥，沒有罪惡，沒有悲傷，因為我的心從未犯過錯。犯錯的是，我的舌頭。

世界告訴我們，人類歷史不斷重複，沒有什麼改變。

然而，在我們目前經驗的人類苦難歷史中，發生奇妙的事。

人們彼此愈來愈接近。

感謝現代科技和社會媒體，他們日復一日，互相交談，從世界一個角落到另一個角落。

此舉為我們打開新的大門，給予我們新希望。

為我們彼此開啟心胸。人們彼此以愛進入心靈。偏見融化……

儘管技術高度發展，人性道德和倫理卻一再墜落到無法容許的程度。

我的書是告誡和提醒我們是誰。一個偉大的文明。我的書是人性善良及其存在的證明。

親愛的讀者，我始終與你同在。親愛的讀者，我愛你們。

# 目次

自序 Preface　003

可能是最後的咖啡 It could be the last coffee　008

敘利亞在哭泣 Syria is crying　010

最後的火焰 The last flame　014

你偷我 You stole me　016

我聽到他們的話 I have listened to their words　018

無人幫助 Nobody Helps　021

真理 The truth　023

灰心 Lost hearts　025

風在旋轉 The wind whirls　028

人在哪裡 Where are the people　030

其他人 Other people　032

邪念回收者 Recyclers of evil　033

寫給敍利亞來的年輕人
Written for the young man from Syria　036

純真的照片 The photo of innocence　040

我們的信 Our letters　042

吠 Barking　046

科隆猶太人公墓 Jewish cemetery in Köln　049

明天的夢想 The dream of tomorrow　051

戰友 War friend　054

悲傷 The sadness　057

死於心臟手術 Died at heart surgery　058

存在的混沌 Existential chaos　060

夢 Dream　062

彩虹暗藏自己 Hide yourself rainbow　064

同樣顫抖驚醒我們 The same shiver awakes us　067

我們 We　069

人生 Life　070

祕密 Secret　072

死神來臨 Death is coming　073

我已忘掉你 I forgot you　075

為我們 For us　077

沉默 The silence　079

瑪麗亞的眼睛 Maria's eyes　080

在墓地 At the cemetery　081

今晨我心逃逸 This morning my heart fled　083


關於詩人 About the Poet　085

關於譯者 About the Translator　086

# 可能是最後的咖啡

馬哈穆德・德維希

在轟炸下

在恨如雨下喝咖啡

唯一繼續持有

且快樂有趣的事是,

在他住宿的

混凝土瓦礫間

喝咖啡時

水慢慢開始煮開,

咖啡香味,

使他

感到幸福

這日子,

永遠

不會回來。

不再啦，

但他總是在

咖啡裡回味這些日子。

他甚至想

要做最後一件事

用炸彈

把他製成碎肉。

# 敍利亞在哭泣

如果我是老鷹

寬寬闊闊的翅膀

會帶我到那

沒有人想去的地方。

在那裡，每天早上黑暗如夜。

男人殘殺男人，男人呀。

淚流成河

血比各地還要紅。

孩子在哭父

母親在哭兒。

哲人為真理而哭泣

沒有人和和氣氣

或有好心情離開那裡。

大馬士革玫瑰不再芬芳
戀人也不會為愛嘆息。
靜靜的多馬之門*，
已毀於一旦。
那裡曾經是人民彼此
約會談情說愛地方，
門沒啦，再也沒有啦。
人民不見啦
他們都走掉啦。
無人找得到地方約會。
無人在清真寺
甚至在教堂裡禱告。
人的自尊被踐踏

傷不到任何人。

那裡有美目灰白

埋在土裡。

但我想去那裡

通過無人的街道

我想走到那裡

唱歌和祈禱。

請不要互相殘殺

請不要再殺我們。

請回家吧孩子，

因為沒有你

你母親

就心死了。

因為玫瑰

無刺就不能存在。

而你一定知道

最好是死在自家

門口

握著可愛的手，

勝於死在

異地。

敘利亞在哭泣

請回家吧，

失去孩子會傷害我

傷到我自己的心。

*註：多馬之門（Bab Tuma）是敘利亞首都大馬士
　　革古城牆上的一座城門，也是早期基督教的
　　地理地標，取名自耶穌十二門徒之一多馬。

# 最後的火焰

在萬事平靜之前

最後的火焰燃燒著，

煙慢慢熄滅，

我的良知正在伸張，

使我悲不自勝。

為什麼總是非燃燒不可

在任何事情變化之前

像灰燼氣味嗎？

難道燃燒

就是某種變化？

燃燒掉

時間，

情感，

心，

人，

在我們走之前

生命燃燒最後的火焰。

# 你偷我

把我帶入你的夢中，
你手上長滿青苔，
把我帶進洞窟，
我們從哪裡來
就又回到那裡去，
我們野生男女，
奔向自然，本來面貌
不是我們想像那樣。
把我帶到你有火的地方
在你裸身躺臥的
永恆之火旁邊，熱，
我正在孕育你的夢想
和你的新世界。
你帶我來

到霧靄，

當做天使

你把我綑在黑暗中

不窺探謊言，

變得更強壯。

我狂笑

真是快樂的女人……

你帶我，

你帶著我，

你總是保護我

免於謊言的世界

我們只有夢想

而我們不活在那裡。

# 我聽到他們的話

我聽到他們的話

傷透已經苦惱的心。

我聽到他們開口喊叫聲

他們沒有告訴任何人，

保留隱而不宣。

我聽到喊叫聲

塞住耳朵，

他們的話，

還有虛耗的希望，

他們心之所及

把悲傷轉化為故事。

我看到他們掉淚，

用手

逐一擦掉。

我看到他們腿在顫抖

跌跌撞撞，

看到年輕人的

折磨和恐懼，

被當做牲禮的羊群。

他們低頭

不出聲

在掉眼淚

逝矣，而，

美麗青草在揮手。

像綿羊，

狼來抓，

銳牙咬進喉嚨，

我聽到，

嘆息聲拋向天空。

我在他們眼裡看到生命

發現充滿悲傷。

# 無人幫助

無人幫助我們，

無人理解

無人感到痛苦

無人每天

心中

雨淋淋。

無人失去太陽

以如此藝術方式活著，

被幻想包圍

像羊放牧

在人民失去自尊的地方，

上方總是籠罩烏雲。

無人，無人有那麼多力氣

埋葬他們的兒女。

無人有那麼多耐心和希望

在對抗巴勒斯坦人的邪惡中取勝。

# 真理

婦女懷著痛苦

與瞭然的真理同埋，

在男人釘上十字架時，

孩子們愛跟著她，

她指給他們看

血腥恐懼的樣子，

她跟隨他們到處奔波。

小小乳房餵養他們

引導他們

走過夢想，

她不為他們恐懼。

女人懷著痛苦

與真理同埋

在父親釘上十字架時

她無言

好像她的話

已死在森林中

他們永遠不會

瞭解。

受傷的天空

為她哭泣

真誠愛十字架上的女人。

女人懷著真理

永遠埋葬

在男人的腳下。

# 灰心

我處在那

血淚流淌的地方，

父母在那裡

被河流沖走，

孩子獨自

在岸上哭泣，

又傷心又飢餓，

只有黑夜，

來安慰，

只有無盡的惡夢。

我處在那

草木不生的地方

悲慘根深傷重。

我處在那

對滿佈傷痕的地面

撒愛的地方，

親人在找失落

無蹤的親人。

我想到那裡去

撫慰全部人類的

悲傷。

我想在那裡種植

希望之花

利用毀壞房屋所在

失修的籬笆

眼前一片空無。

我想去看看

希望之花如何生長。

第一批花卉出現

長出苞蕾呼喊：

夠啦夠啦，

淚水如雨下夠啦。

我想在那裡

尋找灰心的人

撫慰他們的痛苦。

# 風在旋轉

心靈呼叫，

思想正窒息中

融入謊言裡，

這時心靈呼叫是在求真相。

黑風發癢、怒吼且流竄

進入耳朵，塞在我們思想裡。

思想一出生，美麗又純潔，

黑風就偷走了，

就在怒吼流竄中

帶去給蛇魔，

填熱胃，

蛇魔把思想扔在柴堆上。

偷走我們最後蛋糕！

最後一塊！

我們餓死了，

心靈

在痛哭

逃離謊言

尋找死亡真相。

黑風怒吼流竄，

滿足蛇魔。

風在旋轉。

# 人在哪裡

今晚我獨自走在

生活街道上，

尋找我的小巷

尋找我的道路。

霧和我同在街上，

尋找人民

在每個陰影裡

可能有人。

用心和眼睛找，

人在哪裡

就消失在那裡。

空無人跡的街上

看不到任何人

只有一大堆活死人醒著。

沒人，

所有人民都死了，

我孤孤單單，快瘋了。

不知道都在哪裡，

躲在哪裡

也許是彼此

全部殺光。

# 其他人

我該怎麼哄自己

萬事美好，

直到有幾千人瞬間

在洪水中淹死。

我們騎上牝馬

天天增加殘酷無情，

牝馬卻正在自尊成長。

我們的心已變麻木

在呼嘯的海洋上

我們無憂無慮，冷漠游泳。

神在考驗我們無法堅持，

也許有其他人會

至少。

# 邪念回收者

邪念比往常更深入腦內。

一定是植根在心中，

一定是築巢在裡面

緩慢而安全成長

進入我們胃部

從嘴裡

冒出來

從眼裡噴出來，

從耳裡嘶嘶出聲，

從皮膚

和每個毛孔

尖叫。

邪念佔領

整個人，

一瞬間

人不再是人

甚至不是魔鬼，

只是邪念，愚蠢的邪念。

笨、俗、無腦

從出生就不是人樣，

我們從某處撿來，

從生活上某一路徑

我弄不清楚何時何地

找到的

仔細加以看管。

每個人在自己路上

會邂逅那髒物，撿起來。
我們就是邪念回收者
在我們心裡一再冒出，
始終以新的形式
從我們外表爆出來。

# 寫給敍利亞來的年輕人

今天清早，

我還有母親和妹妹，

現在是孤單一人。

今天清早，太陽有感覺

我想再活一天，

今早我餓了

夢想一片麵包

和一點點溫暖

但不單獨吃，

要與母親

和妹妹分享

慢慢咀嚼到明天

讓我醒來

迎接新的早晨，
即使炸彈如雨落下
我會高興看到
母親和妹妹在笑。
現在她們死啦。
她們在那裡，
躺在心愛的國家
那國家不愛我們。
我在心裡尋找悲傷，
但不見啦。
已經死啦，
寂靜無聲。
我但願能哭出聲來，

也許她們會醒來安慰我，

但在我生命裡什麼都沒啦，

所有感覺都消失啦。

我也死啦，

我只是好像活坐在這裡，

即使全世界都在更新

很美，但不能

補綴那心身的

裂縫

沒有人可以評斷

那些罪行，這個邪惡

是人對人所作所為。

而其他人從遠處旁觀

竟說「感謝神，幸好不是
發生在我們身上。」

# 純真的照片

渴望純真

和自由良知

除了心在臉上

別無其他

重量非常輕

幾乎像天堂鳥的羽毛

眼睛看來無可懷疑

充滿信心

在世界上

誰還未領略痛苦呢

今天我要眼睛

不再是攝影

只反映

其中新的邪惡世界
我也不想再要了
寧願在記憶中保留
此光無虛榮
此世沒有艱苦。

# 我們的信

一看到你

我心旌動蕩

就像地震

我想寫信向你

傾訴一切

經過

我自己的

一種道德檢肅，

使我癱瘓了。

我該如何是好？

我自訂

界限和規範，

何者可為或不可為。

我是自己的法官

要宣判

自己死刑，

餓死，

餓於愛情。

我只要想到

你不

再給我

寫信，

就像你用手

摀住我的口

阻絕呼吸。

神呀，我

還有藥可治嗎？

也許只有我們的信。

說吧，是誰強迫你告訴我

你還存在、還在呼吸？

你也和我一樣瘋狂，

從何時開始

你就在偷

我的思想和話語，

天知道

而我現在才發覺。

我的生活

很平靜，

但最糟的是

我想到的一切

從腦海裡

必須立即刪除。

所以，

去掉我所有的話

和思想，得分。

我們循未知方向

活下去，

但在某一點

相遇。

那就是

當你在讀我的信

我在讀你信的時候。

# 吠

如果我們今天像狗吠

成什麼體統

誰會偶爾這樣吠。

只好檢查

他們是否活人。

因為

有些人

如果不吠

甚至會沒命。

和平與沉默

像是他們的墳墓。

讓我們像狗那樣吠吧

為爭骨頭而吠，

看誰大聲。

有些會垂下尾巴，

跑到另一邊

傷心沉默，

觀察我們的注意力和耐性

潛近又來搶我們，

可是忘記我們的牙齒，

更白更尖銳，

更憤怒

更真實又更大，

因為失望的緣故。

我知道甚至人群中有這類狗。

搖晃的牙齒，

又小又虛張聲勢，

逐一掉落，

他們無齒繼續吠，

悲乎！

# 科隆猶太人公墓

墳墓在睡覺，

被遺忘而成為永恆。

註定要密封，

硬幣覆在眼上。

靜極！

大家在哪裡？

人在哪裡？

只有灰塵增多

成為守衛，

沒有花，

一丁點都沒有。

只剩下幾顆小卵石

證明有人來過

參拜墓地。

墓園訪客現在

哪裡去啦？

埋在其他城鎮嗎？

愛妳想要愛的人

妳也不得不離開他。

這書上有寫。

我想明天

帶花來，

點燃蠟燭，

把大家叫醒。

讓墓園再度復活

把故事告訴我

如果有結束，

就說到完。

# 明天的夢想

今天

多聞一次空氣，

明天會是

謊言的氣味。

現在

多碰觸一次樹木，

因為明天

就只是夢想。

今天

多親吻一次你的孩子，

明天可能

很快失去生命

被拋棄。

當炸彈成排紛飛

我們心碎，俯身哭泣，

當灰塵瞎掉我們眼睛

我們生命就此全滅

那就不用哭啦！

眼淚不會擦拭掉

人的獸性之火。

起來，走吧，

天空總是

比地球更美。

天空不是黑色，

不會像火

燃燒。

地球上美麗萬物

已移向天堂

地球和平

只是明天的夢想。

無論夢到誰，都隱而不見！

# 戰友

朋友

幫我再拍一張照片，

也許是最後一次。

對我多一次記憶，

趁我還活著

為你，為你。

朋友

不要忘記我，

如果戰後

還能平安活著

快快樂樂。

如果還能平安呼吸

而我沒啦

幫我帶一張照片

給我媽

一張給老爸。

幫我擁抱他們，

伴我棺木。

幫他們永生的兒子

給他們發訊息。

我如今在最美寶座上。

朋友

請拍最後一張照片

隨身攜帶，

也許你還會需要我

即使你倒下，

失去四肢

那時戰爭在唱

凱旋曲。

如果炸彈瞎掉你的眼睛

我會幫你逃出地獄

消失無蹤。

朋友

為我拍最後一張照片。

# 悲傷

（印度賤民）

有時候我會自問

神創造我

到底是何目的？

也許只是

要對無辜受害者

哀悼和流淚

作為神賜關注，

與死者會合

和他們一起邁步

走向天堂……

# 死於心臟手術

我曾經很接近

一位匿名女性的死亡，

她獨自躺在病房裡。

沒有人願意

如此接近死亡。

但我去了

對她懷著敬意

和愛心。

片刻間我偷偷哭了，

她如此孤零零，在病房裡。

我輕輕掀開

她失去生命的身體

再看一遍

她死亡的眼睛，

曾經是多麼活躍開朗，

好像要告訴我

我還活著呢。

她的眼睛在哀悼自己。

我見過。

我拍拍她已經僵冷的手臂，

向她道歉，

為了我不得不對她施加痛苦

從她身上

拔下心律調整器電線。

「這無礙，」她告訴我

對我笑

在天堂外。

# 存在的混沌

潛入混沌裡

一如全盤順勢

簡單

容易消化

不要問太多

不要思考

只要活著

進入已知軌跡

最終

在我們前頭那些人

並沒有更好，

準備度餘生吧

在死之前

看日落。

但是太陽的公墓在何處

我要去那裡，也在我走之前。

但是群星的公墓在何處

星星還會照耀我們。

其他宇宙在何處

何者會悼念我們。

# 夢

我夢到

和平

已死,

我夢到

無人

為之傷心。

我夢到人民

彼此偷心,

真理窺探謊言面貌

一個接一個疑慮。

我夢到鬥獸場

獅子在接吻,

嗅花,萬無一失

正開心。

我夢到螞蟻

長成巨人，

我夢到下雨

從大而降，

我夢到人都很高，

我夢到做夢，

在和平宇宙中醒來，

和平從未消失，

我只夢到我瘋啦。

# 彩虹暗藏自己

我正要走，你也要走，他們都要走

我們一起並肩走吧

沒有誰聽誰的話。

怎麼啦，心靈不相互交談嗎？

怎麼啦，他們不談論一切，

談論悲傷，談論暗藏的眼淚，

每個人在淚一滴落就帶走，

在雲端

剛好等到滴下來

心想加以破碎

分散全世界。

分給每人一點點心靈。

有何不可？

當心靈大且永久。

何不？

我的心靈想在夜裡

從這裡跳躍到墨西哥，

或到敘利亞，

在那裡許多母親看守著死嬰

在那裡姊妹在唱傷心的歌，

在那裡你到處看不到

豔麗彩虹和快樂。

雲會立即加以驅散

懷著恐懼說：

暗藏你！至少你！

有一天我們還會需要你，

暗藏你，我的彩虹，

因為那時候

我們會單獨留下。

太陽和雲。

誰會讚賞我們？

有其他孩子會出生

許多遠處的水會流到某處

不知道他們會不會來找我們，

我們每天晚上都在

靜靜等待

新生命

和一些新人類。

暗藏你，我的彩虹呀，

暗藏你不讓人看見。

# 同樣顫抖驚醒我們

感覺妳在想念我，
我愛妳的忐忑不安
和空虛感，
妳心煩時會飄向我
像沉著後的微風。
我愛妳的實體，
妳的嘆息溫暖我
妳的眼睛是兩隻驚慌的鹿。
我愛尾隨妳的恐懼，
只是妳向來不願承認。
昨天沒有，
明天沒有，
今天也沒有。

也許，也許，也許有一天，

有一天早上，妳感覺

同樣顫抖驚醒我們，

嚇到我們，

竊據我們的安寧

且為我們帶來

新的希望。

# 我們

我們沒有記憶，

回顧時，只有追憶。

我們沒有摟抱身體。

沒有，只有在擁抱中顫抖的心靈，

在彼此相殺時的懷念。

我們被生命分離，

那不是生活，

只是夢

和幻想

我們在做夢

只有一點點

人類幸福。

# 人生

人生有時候

像落葉的樺樹，

透明又灰白，

就像鳥鳴

讓人想起新春

正是新的開始。

一起頭就永不終止，

萬事開頭

一而再，

持續不絕。

春天到

接二連三

等候真美好。

鳥都知道，
蝴蝶知道
蜜蜂也知道。

# 祕密

眼睛隱藏祕密

只片刻

即炯炯發亮

隱藏不住，

等待一次機會

再現

安全和不被注意

白天的光

太陽會給溫暖。

# 死神來臨

蠟燭搖晃

又一夜

在黎明熄滅。

天上無星

也無陽光醒來。

失竊的臉和失蹤的

刺眼的光。

心丟進火裡。

男人躺在

火葬柴堆上

經驗。

知識。

愛與恨。

隨他一起焚化

生命在火中燃燒

生命在痛苦火中誕生。

非自願而來，

非自願而去，

離開此

世界。

# 我已忘掉你

石頭在胸口，

淚在眼裡，

夜在爛，

你在我的相思裡。

孤男

站在雨中，

狗在桶內

被踐踏的花在哭泣。

最後的煙飄散，

有人跑走，

我心跳激烈，

愈來愈強，愈強

有影子經過，

我原以為是你，

我用手捂嘴

把火籠深掩在

雨濕的皮膚下。

淚垂在臉上，

狗跑去別地方，

孤男和別人

相見擁抱，

花又傷心哭泣

石頭變沙，

淚從眼中蒸發

影子消失

像黑暗在黑暗中

我心停止跳動

我已忘掉你。

# 為我們

今早

我把祕密對神低語

沒人聽到

讓祂知道只有我們

今早

我種植愛情

任其成長

隱藏在神眼裡

今早我請求河流

容我走進去

冷卻我

正熾熱的心

今早

我請求鳥用翅膀

帶我到你身邊

今早

我流兩滴淚

為我們。

# 沉默

沉默靜到

沒什麼可怕。

事件在另一方面已給我們

彼此啟示，精采的

四手彈奏鋼琴曲，

兩體一心。

這首歌只演奏一次

這感覺只產生一次。

愛永遠密封。

隱藏在沉默中。

呼吸。

# 瑪麗亞的眼睛

瑪麗亞的眼睛

沒成長，

還是孩子樣。

瑪麗亞的眼睛還沒搬家，

依然在她童年的

花園大門玩

再也沒有人會把她誘走，

留下她心愛的丁香。

因為瑪麗亞的眼睛一直

與記憶中的補丁娃娃，

她的愛慕也是她的明星一起玩。

# 在墓地

土剛剛被挖走

另一個心靈移入。

柔軟的枕頭永遠在，

等待永恆安息者。

每一滴眼淚都悶在裡面，

每一個希望都被擊潰。

濕透那麼多眼淚

內藏有海洋，

每位安息者

夢見天堂。

但裡面真正是什麼

講哪一種

語言，

永遠是祕密

直到我們倒下

進入墓地那一天，

那時我們家人在

耐性祈禱。

# 今晨我心逃逸

今晨

我心離開你逃逸

一句話都不說，

今晨

我看到心的血跡

也看到如何攀上天空

與陽光在一起。

今晨

我的身體

留有裂開的胸口

苦淚從眼睛滴下來

我的手和嘴唇

與無言的靈魂廝守，

心逃逸，

我聽到說話聲

來自上方：

把一切都埋葬吧，

我在這裡躺著不動

看似木乃伊

不幸

我自問

該把心叫

回來嗎

不然再試一次

並無意義。

# 關於詩人

　　出生於塞爾維亞國新帕扎爾市（Novi Pazar），現住德國，以雙語寫作，有三個孩子。2013年開始寫詩，已出版兩本詩集。第一本《從我胸腔喊出的一首詩》（Ein Gedicht schreit auf aus meiner Brust），2016年在柏林出版，第二本《愛與恐懼》（Love and Fear），在塞爾維亞共和國貝爾格萊德市出版。在義大利榮獲過詩獎。詩譯成許多語文，尤其是英文、義大利文、漢文、塞爾維亞文。2018年有英文、義大利文、漢文，以及德文新書將出版。

# 關於譯者

　　李魁賢，1937年生，1953年開始發表詩作，曾任台灣筆會會長，國家文化藝術基金會董事長。現任世界詩人運動組織（Movimiento Poetas del Mundo）副會長。詩被譯成各種語文在日本、韓國、加拿大、紐西蘭、荷蘭、南斯拉夫、羅馬尼亞、印度、希臘、美國、西班牙、巴西、蒙古、俄羅斯、立陶宛、古巴、智利、尼加拉瓜、孟加拉、馬其頓、土耳其、波蘭、塞爾維亞、葡萄牙、馬來西亞、義大利等國發表。

　　出版著作包括《李魁賢詩集》全6冊、《李魁賢文集》全10冊、《李魁賢譯詩集》全8冊、翻譯《歐洲經典詩選》全25冊、《名流詩叢》29冊、《人生拼圖──李魁賢回憶錄》，及其他共二百本。英譯詩集有《愛是我的信仰》、《溫柔的美感》、《島與島之間》、《黃昏時刻》和《存在或不存在》。詩集《黃昏時刻》共有英文、蒙古文、羅馬尼亞文、俄文、西班牙文、法文、韓文、孟加拉文、阿爾巴尼亞文、塞爾維亞文、土耳其文、馬其頓文出版。

　　曾獲韓國亞洲詩人貢獻獎、榮後台灣詩獎、賴和文學獎、行政院文化獎、印度麥氏學會詩人獎、吳三連獎新詩獎、台灣新文學貢獻獎、蒙古文化基金會文化名人獎牌和詩人獎章、蒙古建國八百週年成吉思汗金牌、成吉思汗大學金質獎章和蒙古作家聯盟推廣蒙古文學貢獻獎、真理大學台灣文學家牛津獎、韓國高麗文學獎、孟加拉卡塔克文學獎、馬其頓奈姆·弗拉舍里文學獎、祕魯特里爾塞金獎。

# *Preface*

Poems by Elvira Kujovic

Dear reader, what should I tell you, that you have already not read in another book?

Maybe just some new data about me that are unique, or maybe not, but very familiar to some of you.

I can imagine that there are many people who were born on the same day, so I also hope that those people carry the same love in their hearts as I do.

In this book is my heart, along with my soul.

As you read this book, you will get to know my heart naked.

Naked, without shame, without sin, without grief, because my heart has never sinned. But my tongue did.

The world teaches us that the history of humanity is

untiringly repeating and there is nothing to change.

Nevertheless, in this painful history of humanity, which we are currently experiencing, is happening a wonderful thing.

People are getting closer to each other.

Thanks to modern technology and social media, they talk to each other day in and day out, from one corner of the world to the other.

This opens new doors for us and gives us new hopes.

It opens our hearts for one another. People look each other with love into their souls. Prejudices melt away...

Despite the highest development of technology, human morality and ethical visions fall repeatedly under

the limit of allowance.

My book is the admonition and the reminder of who we are. A great civilization. My book is a proof of human goodness and its existence.

Dear readers, I am always with you. Dear readers, I love you.

*Elvira Kujovic*

# *It could be the last coffee*

Mahmud Dervish drank his coffee

under the bombardment

under the rain of hatred

but the only thing he still had

and what was his pleasure and fun,

was drinking of coffee

between the concrete ruin

in which he lived,

the water that slowly began to boil

and the smell of coffee,

which reminded him

of the happiness

and the days

which will never

came back,

never again,

but he always found

those days in his coffee.

Even wanted it to be

the last thing he had,

while the bombs

of him the mince made.

# Syria is crying

If I were an eagle

my wide wings

would carry me there,

where nobody wants to go.

There, were every morning dark is as an evening,

there were the man kills the man, oh man,

there were the tears are flowing as a river

and blood is more red as usual.

There were the child is crying for the father

and for her son, is crying a mother,

a wise man is crying for the truth

and nobody leaving there in the peace

or in the good mood.

Damascus roses are not smelling any more

and the lovers do not lovingly sigh,

there where the gate Bab –Tuma

silent is, and destroyed.

There, where once the people met

each other and loved,

but there is no one

and all the people are disappeared

they are all gone.

Nobody met each other nowhere,

not in the mosque

even in the church to pray.

There is human pride treading

and it, does not hurt anyone.

There, are nice eyes grey,

buried in the clay.

But I want to go there

through empty street

I want to walk there and sing

the love songs and prayer.

Please don't kill each other

please don't kill us any more.

Please come back at home my child,

because without you,

your mother's heart

is already dead.

The roses can not exist

without briar,

and you have to know

that is better to die

on the doorstep of your own

holding a lovely hand,

than to die in the foreign land.

Syria cries and bags

please come back at home

without my children is hurting me

the heart of my own.

# The last flame

The last flame burns

Before everything

calms down,

the smoke dies slowly,

my conscience is spreading,

and the sorrow is overwhelming me.

Why does it always have to burn

and smell like the ash

before anything changes?

Is the burning

some kind of

a change?

The burning

of the time,

of the feelings,

of the heart,

and a man.

The last flame

of life burns

before we go.

*2015*

# *You stole me*

You brought me into your dream,

on your hands overgrown with moss,

you brought me into the cave,

where we come from

and where we return again,

we wild women and man,

with an urge for nature but so as it is

and not for the kind we imagine.

You brought me to your fireplace

next to your eternal fire to lie

naked and hot,

and I'm giving birth to your dreams

and your new worlds.

You brought me

to the cloud of fog,

as an angel

and you bind me in black

not to look in the lie,

but to become stronger.

And I laugh with the laughter

of a crazy and happy woman ...

You brought me,

you took me with you,

you've always protect me

from the world of the lies

which we only dream

and which we do not live.

# *I have listened to their words*

I have listened to their words which

saddened my already afflicted heart.

I listened to the cries of their lips

which they did not anybody tell,

hidden and unspoken they stayed.

I listened to the cry

which the ears suffocate,

their words,

and exhausted hope too,

which their heart reached

and transmutes the sadness into the Story.

I watched their tears fall down,

and their hands

wiping them one by one.

I saw a shiver in their legs

which makes them fall,

watching the persecution and the fear

of the young human beings,

taken as the herd of the Kurban rams.

They bent their heads

without voice and

their tears fell,

they died, while,

the beautiful grass waved.

Like the sheep,

the wolf grabbed them,

bit its teeth

into their throat and I listened,

as their sighs went in the sky.

I saw their life in their eyes

and a lot of sadness found.

# *Nobody Helps*

Nobody helps us,

nobody understands

nobody does feel the pain

nobody has the rain

every day

in their hearts.

Nobody lost the sun

in such artistic way to live,

surrounded by a fance

like sheep in a field

where the people lost their pride,

above them, hangs always black cloud.

Nobody, nobody has so much strength

in the burying of their daughters and sons.

Nobody has so much patience and hope to win,

Against evil as Palestine people.

# *The truth*

Women pregnant with pain

buried,

with the naked truth

on the man's cross crucified,

by her children, are loved her heels,

she gave them the way,

by bloody fear

she walked behind them,

a little breast fed them

through dreams she lead them,

fearless she stood for them.

The woman pregnant with pain,

on the father's cross crucified,

In her mouth the word died.

Her bruised sky for her cries

and loves her faithfully.

Woman pregnant

with the pain buried

with the naked truth,

loves forever.

# *Lost hearts*

My place is there

where the bloody tears go,

where father and mother

down the river flow,

and the child cries

on the bank alone,

miserable and hungry,

and only the dark night,

carries the alleviation,

only an endless black dream.

My place is there

where the grass ceased to grow

and misery spreads roots and hurts.

My place is there

to spill love on earth

full of wounds,

where a beloved seeks for the beloved

missing without a trace.

There I want to be.

all the human sorrows

to soothe.

There I want to plant

the flowers of hope

by the sad fence

where the houses are destroyed

and the eyes are looking at the emptiness.

I want to see how

the flowers of hope grow.

The first flowers appear

and the buds shout:

Enough is enough,

enough of the rain of tears.

There I want

lost hearts to seek

and their pain to soothe.

*2015*

# *The wind whirls*

The cry of the soul,

thoughts are suffocating

in a lie are melting,

while the cry of the soul seeks for the truth.

The black wind tickles, roars and flows

enters the ears and our thoughts it chokes.

As soon as born, beautiful and pure,

the black wind steals them

while roaring and flowing

brings them to the serpent,

to her hot maw,

on the pyre

it throws.

Steals our last cake!

The last one!

We die hungry,

while the cry

of the soul

flees from the lie

and seeks the truth in the death.

The black wind roars and flows,

and satisfies the serpent.

The wind whirls.

*2016*

# *Where are the people*

On the street of life

I walk alone tonight,

searching for my alley

searching for my way.

The fog and me

are on the street,

looking for the people,

in every shadow

could somebody be.

Where are the people

with the heart and with eyes,

where they disappear,

where have they gone?

Empty streets

I cannot anybody see

only a mass of zombies

awakening.

There is no one,

all the people are dead,

I am alone and becoming mad.

I wonder where they are,

Where they hid

maybe each other

they all killed.

*2016*

# *Other people*

How should I lie to me

everything will be good,

until the people die in the flood

thousands in minute.


And we ride on the mare of inhumanity

which every day become bigger,

she is growing with pride.


Our hearts have we turned into wood

above the screaming oceans

we heedlessly, swim callous.

This God test we will not insist,

maybe any other people

at least.

09.08.2015

# Recyclers of evil

The evil lives deeper than just in the head.

it must have left the roots in the heart,

it must have nested in it

slowly and safely it grows

into our stomach so that

it would come out

from our mouth

from the eyes it will spout,

from the ears it will hiss,

from the skin

and each pore

it will scream.

The evil possesses

the man in a whole,

and at one moment

a man is no longer a man

not even a devil anymore,

just evil, unintelligent evil.

Stupid, vulgar, low thoughts

are not man-like from his birth,

we collect them from somewhere,

from one of the paths, of our life.

I have no idea when and where

we have found it

and carefully watch them.

Each of us on our way comes

across that dirt and picks it up.

We are the recyclers of evil

which again and again raises in us,

but always in the new shape

it bursts from our skin.

*2017*

# *Written for the young man from Syria*

This morning early,

I had a mother and a sister,

and now I am alone,

this morning early, the sun had a sense

and I wanted to live another day more,

this morning I was hungry

and dreamed a piece of bread

and a kitten warm

but not to eat it alone,

with my mother

and my sister to share it

and slowly chew it

until tomorrow

so that I could wake up

and meet the new morning.

Even if the bombs fell like the rain

I was happy when I saw

that my mother and my sister smiled,

now they are dead.

there they are,

lying on the beloved country

which us didn't love.

I seek for sorrow

in my heart,

but it's gone.

It has died,

it is silent.

I wish I could cry,

maybe they would wake up

to console me,

but in me lives nothing anymore,

all the feelings are gone.

I am also dead,

I am just sitting here as alive,

and even if the whole world renews

and be beautiful, it could not

patch that cleavage

of the soul and the body

and no one could justify

these misdeeds, this evil

which people to people do.

While the others watch from the distance

And say " Thanks God it's not

happening to us."

2017

# The photo of innocence

Longing for innocence

And the free consciences

Nothing is there

Only the heart in the face

A very light weight

Almost like a feather of paradise bird

And the eyes look unsuspected

And full of confidence

In the world

Which knows no pain yet

Today I want my eyes

No more photography

Than it will reflect

The new evil world in them

And I do not want it anymore

I'd rather be kept in my memory

This lightness without vanity

This world without bitterness.

# *Our letters*

Just the glance of you

shakes my chest

like the earthquake

and everything

I want to write to you

goes through

a kind of my own

moral censorship,

which cripples me.

What should I do?

I set up to my own

boundaries and norms,

what could be or not.

I am a judge for me alone

and want to condemn

myself to death,

death of hunger,

hunger of love.

If I only think about

that you are not

writing to me

anymore,

It is like you put your hand

on my mouth

and take my breath.

What's the medicine

for me, my God?

Perhaps only our letters,

say, who compelled you

to show me that you exist and breath?

You who is crazy as I am too

you are stealing

my thoughts and words

since when,

God knows

and I find it out just now.

There was my life

was very quiet,

but worst of all is that

everything what I think

I must immediately delete

from my mind.

And so,

went all my words

and thoughts, in a score.

Our lives go

in unknown directions,

but at one point

they meet themselves.

And that is when

you read my letters

and I read yours.

*2017*

# *Barking*

What would it be like

if we today bark

like dogs

who sometimes bark

just like that,

only to check

if they are alive.

Because there are

some of them

who, if don't bark

don't even live.

Peace and silence

are like a grave to them.

Let's bark as if we are the dogs

barking over the bone,

and whose is bigger.

Some of they will bend their tails,

and run to the other side

miserably silent,

watching for our attention and patience

lurking at us to bounce on us again,

but forgetting that our teeth,

are whiter and sharper,

and anger

realer and bigger,

because disappointment yields it.

I know such dogs even among men,

their shaky teeth,

of small and vile frauds,

fall one by one,

and they continue toothless to bark,

miserable.

*2017*

# Jewish cemetery in Köln

The graves are sleeping,

forgotten and eternal.

Destinies sealed,

coins on the eyes.

Silence!

Where are everybody?

Where are the people?

Only the dust grows

and changes into the guard

there are no flowers,

not even a few.

Just some jackstones left

to testify that someone came

and visited the graves.

And where are the gone by

graveyard visitors now?

Buried at some other town?

Love whom ever you want

you will have to leave him.

That's written in the book.

I want tomorrow,

to bring the flowers,

to light the candles,

let everybody wake up.

let the graveyard live again

and tells me its story

if there is an end,

to the end.

# The dream of tomorrow

Smell today

one more the air,

tomorrow it will be

the smell of the lie.

Touch the trees

one more now,

because tomorrow

it will be only a dream.

Kiss today one more time

your child,

maybe tomorrow

it's quickly gone and abandoned

from the life.

When the bombs are flying in the deep

and our hearts breaks and bends and weep,

when the dust blinds our eyes

all disappears so as our life

then do not cry!

The tears will not erase

the fire of human beast.

Get up and go,

the sky has always been more

beautiful than the earth.

It is not black,

it does not burns

like a fire.

Everything beautiful

from the earth

has been to the heaven moved

and an earth in peace

is the only a dream

of tomorrow.

Whoever will it dream,

is hidden from us!

# *War friend*

Make just one more picture of me

my friend,

maybe it's the last one.

Make one more memory at me,

while I'm still alive

for you, for you.

Do not forget me

my friends,

if after the war

the peace is alive

again and the joy.

If the peace is breathing again

and I am not.

Take a picture of me

for my mother

and one for the old father.

Send them a hug from me,

together with my coffin.

Send them the message

from their ever-living son.

I am now on the most beautiful throne.

Please make just one last photo

of me my friend

and always carry it with you,

maybe you will need me

again even if you lie down,

without limbs

while the war is singing

victory songs.

If the bombs blinded your eyes

I will help you out of the Hell

to disappear.

Make just one last photo

of me my friend.

*2017*

# *The sadness*

Sometimes I ask myself

for which purpose

did the god create me?

Maybe just

about the innocent victims

to mourn and tears

as the blessing to shed,

to join the dead

and just take a step with them

to go to paradise.

*2017*

# *Died at heart surgery*

Once I came very close

to the death of an unknown woman,

who lie alone in the hospital room.

Nobody wanted to be

so close to death,

But I went to her

with the respect

and with love.

For a while I cried secretly,

so alone, in her hospital room.

I uncovered gently

her lifeless body

and looked once more

in her dead eyes,

that were so alive and open,

when they wanted to tell me

I'm still alive.

Her eyes mourned for herself.

I have seen that.

I stroked her already cold arm,

I apologized to her,

for pain I would have to do to her

and pulled the pacemaker wires

out of her body.

"It did not hurt her," she told me

and laughed at me

out of paradise.

*2017*

# *Existential chaos*

Dive into the chaos

as all obedient,

be simple

and easy to digest.

Do not ask much

do not think.

just live.

Go into the known trails

at the end

those before us

didn't have any better,

Be ready to pass away

and watch the sunset

before it dies.

But where is the cemetery

of the sun

I would go there,

before I go also.

But where is the cemetery

of the Stars

And will they still shine

after us.

And where are the other universes

Which will mourn for us.

*2017*

# *Dream*

I dreamed

the Peace

was dead,

I dreamed

nobody was

about it sad.

I dreamed the People

stole hearts one another,

the truth looks in the face of the lie

and smokes one joint after the other.

I dreamed of a Colosseum

and in it the lions are kissing,

smell flowers and are nothing missing

they are just happy.

I dreamed of the ants

grew like a giants,

I dreamed of the rain

falling hot from the sky,

I dreamed all people was high,

I dreamed a dream about a dream,

and I woke up in the universe of peace,

which has never disappeared

and I only dreamed,

that I'm mad.

*2017*

# *Hide yourself rainbow*

I'm going, you're going, they're going

we all go alongside each other,

and no one can hear anyone.

How come, the souls do not talk to each other?

How come, they do not talk about everything ,

about their sadness, about their hidden tear,

that everyone carries it

as the drops at the edge of the cloud

just waiting to drop down.

And the heart wants to crack

and divide itself

across the world.

To give everyone a little bit of its soul.

And why not?

When the soul is big and eternal.

Why not?

My soul wants to jump

from here to Mexico at night,

or to Syria where,

mothers keep watch of dead babies

where a sister, sister is singing a song of sorrow,

and where you can´t see the rainbow

colourful and happy anywhere.

The clouds are immediately driving it away

with fear and say,

hide yourself, at least you!

Someday we will need you again,

Hide yourself my rainbow,

because then

we will be left alone .

The Sun and the clouds.

And who will then adore us?

While the other children will be born

a lot of distant water will flow somewhere

we don't know if they will come to us or no

and are we waiting every night

in the silence,

for a new life

and some new people.

Hide yourself my rainbow,

hide yourself from the people.


*2014*

# *The same shiver awakes us*

I feel that you miss me,

and I love your restlessness

and emptiness,

while upset you stream to me

like the breeze through the tranquillity.

I love your body,

your sigh which warms me

and your eyes as two deer's fearful arc.

I love that fear which tails you,

but you never wanted to admit.

Not yesterday,

nor tomorrow,

neither today.

Maybe, maybe, maybe one day,

one morning, when you feel

the same shiver wakes us,

when it startles us,

steals our peace

and arise the new hopes

for us.

*2016*

# *We*

We have no memories,

behind us, will be just remembrances.

We don't have the hugging of the bodies.

Nothing, only our souls

which in the embrace shiver,

and kill each other in the yearn.

We, separated by life,

which it wasn't life,

just a dream

and illusions

we are dreaming

only a little bit of

the humans happiness.

*2017*

# *Life*

Life is sometimes

like a birch without leaves,

transparent and grey,

just the twitter of the birds

recalls on the new springs

and that the new beginnings.

Beginnings never terminate,

everything that begins

again and again,

lasts for ever.

Springs come

one after the other

and it's beautiful to await them.

Each bird knows that,

each Butterfly

and each bee.

*2017*

# Secret

The eye hides the secret

and only for a moment

boldly glitters in it

than hides itself

and waits

for a chance

when it could again

safe and unnoticed

see the light of the day

and the sun

which will warm it.

*2015*

# *Death is coming*

The candle trembles

one more night

and disappeared in the dawn.

Not one star is in the sky

not the one sunray which awakes.

Stolen face and missing light which

bites the eye.

Into the fire thrown the heart.

On the pyre of the dry branches

the man lies.

Experience.

Knowledge.

Love and hate.

Burn with him.

In the fire burns the life

born in the fire of the pains.

Without it's will comes,

without it's will goes,

leaves

this world.

*2016*

# *I forgot you*

Stone in the chest,

tears in the eyes,

night in the tatters,

and you in my thoughts.

The lone man

stood in the rain,

dog was in the bucket

and the trampled flowers cried.

The last smoke fled,

somebody ran away,

and my heart beats strong,

stronger, stronger than ever,

one shadow passed by,

I thought it was yours,

and my hand covered my mouth

and hid my hearth deep under the skin

wet from the rain.

one tear touched my face,

the dog went somewhere,

the lone man met and hugged

somebody,

the flowers cried sadly again

and the stone turned into the sand,

the tear evaporated from the eye

the shadow disappear

like the dark in the dark

my heart stopped beating

and I forgot you.

*2016*

# *For us*

This morning

I whispered my secret to God

That no one hears

And let he only for us know

This morning

I planted our love

And let it grow

Hidden under the eyes of God

This morning I asked the river

To walk in

And cool off my heart

Which is burning

This morning

I asked a bird for a wing

To carry me to you

This morning

I expire two tears

to flow for us.

*2017*

# *The silence*

This silence is too quiet.

There is nothing to fear.

The happening had revealed us each other

in another facet.

That was a fantastic

piano composition for four hands,

two bodies and one soul.

The song is played only once

The feeling is created only once.

Love forever sealed.

Hidden in silence.

Breathes.

*2017*

# *Maria's eyes*

Maria's eyes

have not grown up,

they have remained those of a child.

Maria's eyes have not yet emigrated,

they are still playing

at the garden gate of her childhood

and no human can lure her away again,

to leave her favourite lilac,

Because Maria's eyes are still playing

with the rag doll of their memories,

with her yearning and with her star.

*2017*

# *At the cemetery*

The earth freshly removed

into it another soul carried.

A soft pillow everlasting,

is for the eternal sleeper waiting.

Each tear is suffocated in it,

every hope knocked down.

It soaked so many tears

the ocean is hiding in it.

In it each sleeper

dreams the Heaven.

But what really is in it

and which language

does it speak,

it's imperishable secret

until the day,

we are lied down

into the Kabur*,

while our family prays

for the Sabur**.

*Kabur: grave.
**Sabur: patience.

*2015*

# *This morning my heart fled*

This morning

my heart fled from you

without a word,

this morning

I see its bloody trail

and how it climbs towards the sky

and meet the ray of the sun.

This morning

remains my body

with the hole in the chest to gapes

bitter drops fell from my eyes

my hands and the lips stayed

with wordless soul,

and my heart run away,

I hear it speaking

from above:

Let everything to hell go,

I lie here motionless

looking like a mummy

unfortunate

and I ask myself

shall I call it

to come back,

or to try once again

has no sense.

*2016*

# *About the Poet*

    Elvira Kujovic was born in Novi Pazar, Serbia. She is living in Germany and writing in two languages. She is a mother of three children, started to write in 2013 and issued two books of poems. The first book was published in Berlin in 2016 and bears the name *"Ein Gedicht schreit auf aus meiner Brust"*. The second book is published in Belgrade, Serbia, and bears the name *"Love and Fear"*. Her poetry won an award for poetry in Italy. Her poems

are translated in many world languages, especially English, Italian, Mandarin, and Serbian. Her new books in English, Italian, and Mandarin, as well as her new German book are coming 2018.

## *About the Translator*

Lee Kuei-shien (b. 1937) began to write poems in 1953, became a member of the International Academy of Poets in England in 1976, joined to establish the Taiwan P.E.N. in 1987, was elected as Vice-President and then President, and served as chairman of National Culture and Arts Foundation from 2005 to 2007. Now, he is the Vice President for Asia in Movimiento Poetas del Mumdo (PPdM) . His poems have been translated and published

in Japan, Korea, Canada, New Zealand, Netherlands, Yugoslavia, Romania, India, Greece, USA, Spain, Brazil, Mongolia, Russia, Latvia, Cuba, Chile, Nicaragua, Bangladesh, Macedonia, Turkey Poland, Serbia, Portugal, Malaysia and Italy.

Published works include "Collected Poems" in six volumes, 2001, "Collected Essays" in ten volumes, 2002, "Translated Poems" in eight volumes, 2003, "Anthology of European Poetry" in 25 volumes, 2001~2005, "Elite Poetry Series" in 29 volumes, 2010~2017, and others. His poems in English translation include "Love is my Faith, 1997", "Beauty of Tenderness, 2001", "Between Islands, 2005", "The Hour of Twilight, 2010", "20 Love Poems to

Chile, 2015" and "Existence and Non-existence, 2017". The book "The Hour of Twilight" has been translated into English, Mongol, Romanian, Russian, Spanish, French, Korean, Bengali, Albanian, Serbian, Turkish, and Macedonian languages.

Awarded with Merit of Asian Poet, Korea (1993), Rong-hou Taiwanese Poet Prize (1997), World Poet of the Year 1997, Poets International, India (1998), Poet of the Millennium Award , International poets Academy , India (2000), Lai Ho Literature Prize and Premier Culture Prize , both in Taiwan (2001). He also received the Michael Madhusudan Poet Award from the Michael Madhusudan Academy, India (2002), Wu San-lien Prize in Literature

(2004), Poet Medal from Mongolian Cultural Foundation (2005), Chinggis Khaan Golden Medal for 800 Anniversary of Mongolian State (2006), Oxford Award for Taiwan Writers (2011), Prize of Corea Literature (2013), Kathak Literary Award of Bangladesh (2016), Literary Prize "Naim Frashëri" of Macedonia (2016), "Trilce de Oro" of Peru (2017).

He was nominated by International Poets Academy and Poets International as a candidate for the Nobel Prize in Literature in 2002, 2004 and 2006, respectively.

# Contents

Preface 自序　89

It could be the last coffee 可能是最後的咖啡　92

Syria is crying 敘利亞在哭泣　94

The last flame 最後的火焰　98

You stole me 你偷走　100

I have listened to their words 我聽到他們的話語　102

Nobody Helps 無人幫助　105

The truth 真理　107

Lost hearts 失心　109

The wind whirls 風在旋轉　112

Where are the people 人在哪裡　114

We 我們 155

The same shiver awakes us 同樣顫抖將我們喚醒 153

Hide yourself rainbow 彩虹啊躲藏自己 149

Dream 夢 147

Existential chaos 存在的混沌 145

Died at heart surgery 死於心臟手術 143

The sadness 悲傷 142

War friend 戰友 139

The dream of tomorrow 明天的夢想 136

Jewish cemetery in Köln 科隆猶太人公墓 134

Barking 吠 131

Our letters 我們的信 127

The photo of innocence 純真的照片 125

Written for the young man from Syria
為敘利亞來的年輕人 121

Recyclers of evil 邪惡回收者 118

Other people 其他人 116

Life 人生　156

Secret 祕密　158

Death is coming 死神來臨　159

I forgot you 我已忘掉你　161

For us 為我們　164

The silence 沉默　166

Maria's eyes 瑪麗亞的眼睛　167

At the cemetery 在墓地　168

This morning my heart fled 今晨我心逃逸　170


About the Poet 關於詩人　172

About the Translator 關於譯者　174

獨立作家 PG2026 心洋詩叢29

# 最後的咖啡 The Last Coffee

| | |
|---|---|
| 原 著 / | 艾薇拉・庫喬畢（Elvira Kujovic） |
| 翻 譯 / | 李魁賢（Lee Kuei-shien） |
| 責任編輯 / | 杜國維 |
| 圖文排版 / | 周妤靜 |
| 封面設計 / | 蔡瑋筠 |

出版策劃 / 獨立作家
發 行 人 / 宋政坤
法律顧問 / 毛國樑 律師
製作發行 / 秀威資訊科技股份有限公司
114台北市內湖區瑞光路76巷65號1樓
電話：+886-2-2796-3638 傳真：+886-2-2796-1377
http://www.showwe.com.tw
劃撥帳號 / 19563868 戶名：秀威資訊科技股份有限公司
讀者服務信箱：service@showwe.com.tw
展售門市 / 國家書店（松江門市）
104台北市中山區松江路209號1樓
電話：+886-2-2518-0207 傳真：+886-2-2518-0778
網路訂購 / 秀威網路書店：https://store.showwe.tw
國家網路書店：https://www.govbooks.com.tw

2018年5月 BOD一版
定價：250元

國家圖書館出版品預行編目

最後的咖啡 / 艾薇拉.辜柔維琪(Elvira Kujovic)
著；李魁賢（Lee Kuei-shien）譯. -- 一版. --
臺北市 : 秀威資訊科技, 2018.05
　面；　公分. -- (語言文學類)(名流詩叢；29)
BOD版
譯自 : The last coffee
ISBN 978-986-326-550-4(平裝)

883.3151                                    107004757

# 讀者回函卡

感謝您購買本書，為提升服務品質，請填妥以下資料，將讀者回函卡直接寄回或傳真本公司，收到您的寶貴意見後，我們會收藏記錄及檢討，謝謝！如您需要了解本公司最新出版書目、購書優惠或企劃活動，歡迎您上網查詢或下載相關資料：http:// www.showwe.com.tw

您購買的書名：＿＿＿＿＿＿＿＿＿＿＿＿＿＿＿＿＿＿＿＿＿＿＿

出生日期：＿＿＿＿＿年＿＿＿＿＿月＿＿＿＿＿日

學歷：□高中 (含) 以下　　□大專　　□研究所 (含) 以上

職業：□製造業　□金融業　□資訊業　□軍警　□傳播業　□自由業
　　　□服務業　□公務員　□教職　　□學生　□家管　　□其它

購書地點：□網路書店　□實體書店　□書展　□郵購　□贈閱　□其他

您從何得知本書的消息？

　　□網路書店　□實體書店　□網路搜尋　□電子報　□書訊　□雜誌
　　□傳播媒體　□親友推薦　□網站推薦　□部落格　□其他＿＿＿＿＿

您對本書的評價：(請填代號　1.非常滿意　2.滿意　3.尚可　4.再改進)

　　封面設計＿＿＿　版面編排＿＿＿　內容＿＿＿　文／譯筆＿＿＿　價格＿＿＿

讀完書後您覺得：

　　□很有收穫　□有收穫　□收穫不多　□沒收穫

對我們的建議：＿＿＿＿＿＿＿＿＿＿＿＿＿＿＿＿＿＿＿＿＿＿＿

＿＿＿＿＿＿＿＿＿＿＿＿＿＿＿＿＿＿＿＿＿＿＿＿＿＿＿＿＿＿＿＿

＿＿＿＿＿＿＿＿＿＿＿＿＿＿＿＿＿＿＿＿＿＿＿＿＿＿＿＿＿＿＿＿

＿＿＿＿＿＿＿＿＿＿＿＿＿＿＿＿＿＿＿＿＿＿＿＿＿＿＿＿＿＿＿＿

11466
台北市內湖區瑞光路 76 巷 65 號 1 樓

**秀威資訊科技股份有限公司**　　　收

BOD 數位出版事業部

...........................................................................................

（請沿線對折寄回，謝謝！）

姓　　名：＿＿＿＿＿＿＿＿＿　年齡：＿＿＿＿＿　性別：□女　□男

郵遞區號：□□□□□

地　　址：＿＿＿＿＿＿＿＿＿＿＿＿＿＿＿＿＿＿＿＿＿

聯絡電話：(日) ＿＿＿＿＿＿＿＿＿＿　(夜) ＿＿＿＿＿＿＿＿＿＿

E-mail：＿＿＿＿＿＿＿＿＿＿＿＿＿＿＿＿＿＿＿＿＿